Richard Scarry's
Chipmunk's ABC

By Roberta Miller

Illustrated by Richard Scarry

A GOLDEN BOOK • NEW YORK
Western Publishing Company, Inc., Racine, Wisconsin 53404

W X Y Z

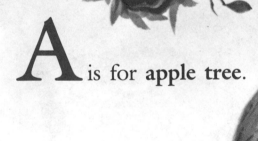

A is for **apple tree**.

B is for **burrow**. Guess who lives in the **burrow** under the apple tree.

Cis for **Chipmunk**. It is **Chipmunk** who lives in the burrow under the apple tree.

Dis for **Donkey**. Chipmunk and **Donkey** have been out picking **daffodils**.

E is for **ears**. Chipmunk's mother washes his **ears**.

F is for **friends**. Chipmunk has many good friends. **Froggie** is a **friend**.

G is for **Goat**.

Goat plays a **game** with Chipmunk.

H

is for **hide-and-seek**. Chipmunk and his
friends **hide** in **holes** and **hedges**.

I is for **ice cream**.

Donkey is serving
ice cream.

J is for **jump**. Froggie **jumps** for **joy**. He loves
ice cream.

K is for **kitchen**. In the **kitchen**, Chipmunk puts the **kettle** on. Mouse slices cheese with a **knife**.

L is for **lake**. Chipmunk and Bunny go sailing on the **lake**. They wear **life jackets**.

M

is for **Mouse**. Mouse has **mumps**. He listens to **music** and has his **meals** in bed.

N is for **net**. Chipmunk catches butterflies in his **net**.

O is for **oboe**. Froggie plays the **oboe**. Donkey drinks from an **orange** cup.

P is for **party**.

Chipmunk loves **parties**. Mouse has gotten over the mumps. He has brought Chipmunk a **present**—a bunch of **pansies**.

Q is for **quilt**. Chipmunk's mother is making a **quilt**.

R is for **river**, where Chipmunk and Donkey are having a swimming **race**.

S is for **swing**.

Chipmunk likes to **swing** almost as much as he likes to **swim**.

T is for **telephone**.

Someone wants to **talk** to Chipmunk.

U

is for **umbrella** to shade Chipmunk's mother from the sun.

V

is for **vacation**. Chipmunk and his mother are at the seashore, staying in a **villa** with a nice **view** of the sea.

W is for **wagon**. Goat pulls the **wagon** and Chipmunk rides. The **weather** is nice, and they have a **watermelon** to eat.

X is a letter. Chipmunk and Bunny play tic-tac-toe with an X and an O.

Y is for **yellow**. **Yellow** flowers grow
in Chipmunk's **yard.**

Z is for **zipper**. Chipmunk **zips** his jacket.
He is going outside to play with his friends.
Have fun, Chipmunk!